P9-DXT-533

Dear Parent:
Your child's love of reading starts here!

Every child learns to read in a different way and at his or her own speed. Some go back and forth between reading levels and read favorite books again and again. Others read through each level in order. You can help your young reader improve and become more confident by encouraging his or her own interests and abilities. From books your child reads with you to the first books he or she reads alone, there are I Can Read Books for every stage of reading:

SHARED READING
Basic language, word repetition, and whimsical illustrations, ideal for sharing with your emergent reader

BEGINNING READING
Short sentences, familiar words, and simple concepts for children eager to read on their own

READING WITH HELP
Engaging stories, longer sentences, and language play for developing readers

READING ALONE
Complex plots, challenging vocabulary, and high-interest topics for the independent reader

I Can Read Books have introduced children to the joy of reading since 1957. Featuring award-winning authors and illustrators and a fabulous cast of beloved characters, I Can Read Books set the standard for beginning readers.

A lifetime of discovery begins with the magical words "I Can Read!"

Visit www.icanread.com for information
on enriching your child's reading experience.

I Can Read® and I Can Read Book® are trademarks of HarperCollins Publishers.

Fancy Nancy: Shoe La La!
Copyright © 2019 by Disney Enterprises, Inc.
All rights reserved. Printed in the United States of America. No part of this book may be used or reproduced in any manner whatsoever without written permission except in the case of brief quotations embodied in critical articles and reviews. For information address HarperCollins Children's Books, a division of HarperCollins Publishers, 195 Broadway, New York, NY 10007.

ISBN 978-0-06-288869-3 (trade bdg.) —ISBN 978-0-06-284387-6 (pbk.)

Book design by Brenda E. Angelilli and Scott Petrower

19 20 21 22 23 LSCC 10 9 8 7 6 5 4 3 2 ❖ First Edition

I Can Read!

BEGINNING 1 READING

Disney Junior

Fancy NANCY

Shoe La La!

Adapted by Victoria Saxon
Based on the episode
by Laurie Israel

Illustrations by the
Disney Storybook
Art Team

HARPER
An Imprint of HarperCollinsPublishers

Ooh la la!

It's a wonderful day to shop.

Mom and I walk down the boulevard.

That's fancy for street.

I look at the fancy things

in the store windows.

I see something I adore!

"Those shoes are more
than beautiful!" I say.
"They're exquisite!"

I ask Mom if I may try them on.

I really, really want them.

I dream about wearing

these exquisite shoes.

Everyone stops to look at me.

Mom asks how much the shoes cost.

She is surprised.

"I'm sorry, sweetie," she says.

"That's too much for shoes
you can't wear every day."

"But they feel like . . . destiny,"

I say.

That's fancy for
these shoes and I
are meant for each other.

Mom and I go home.

When I'm certain things

can't get worse,

I see Grace riding her bike.

She is wearing my red shoes!

I tell Mom that Grace has my shoes.
"I know it's hard seeing your friend
with something you want," Mom says.
But she still won't buy the shoes.

Suddenly, I have an idea.

Maybe Dad will buy me the shoes.

Mom hears me ask Dad.

"Those shoes are forty dollars,"
she says.

"Sorry, Nancy," Dad says.

"My answer is the same as Mom's."

They do not understand how much

I really, really want them!

Then I remember I have money
in my piggy bank.

I am saving for something fancy.

Nothing is more fancy than

bright red shoes!

I count the money in my bank.

I have twenty dollars.

That's not enough!

At lunch, I tell Mom and Dad that I
don't have enough piggy bank money.
Mom says I can earn the rest
by doing extra chores.
I go clean my room.

Mom likes my tidy room.

But she says keeping it clean

is already my job.

I will have to work harder.

Mom and Dad give me

other jobs to do.

I can practically feel

the fancy red shoes on my feet!

I weed Mom's garden.

I walk Mrs. Devine's dog.

I help Dad with the fence.

I polish Grandpa's silverware.

I work very hard.

Finally, I have forty dollars!

I go to the store to buy

the fancy red shoes!

Sacrebleu! Oh no!

I need three dollars more

for sales tax.

I am disappointed.

I thought I had enough

for the fancy red shoes.

I still really, really want them!

As I turn to go,

I see a lady trying on shoes.

They are fabulous and purple!

But the lady isn't sure.

"I'm practically an expert
on shoes," I tell her.
"Those shoes will fancy up
any outfit."

The lady is grateful for my advice.

She decides to buy the shoes.

"Here's a tip," she says.

She gives me three dollars!

"Merci beaucoup!" I say.

That's French for thanks a lot!

She tells me to enjoy

my fancy red shoes.

I am almost one hundred percent

positive I will.

All the hard work was worth it.

My fancy red shoes and I

are together at last!

Fancy Nancy's Fancy Words

These are the fancy words in this book:

Ooh la la—French for wow

Boulevard—street

Exquisite—more than beautiful

Destiny—meant to be

Sacrebleu—French for oh no

Merci beaucoup—French for thanks a lot